Space Cadets to the Rescue

Paul Harrison and Sue Mason

Evans

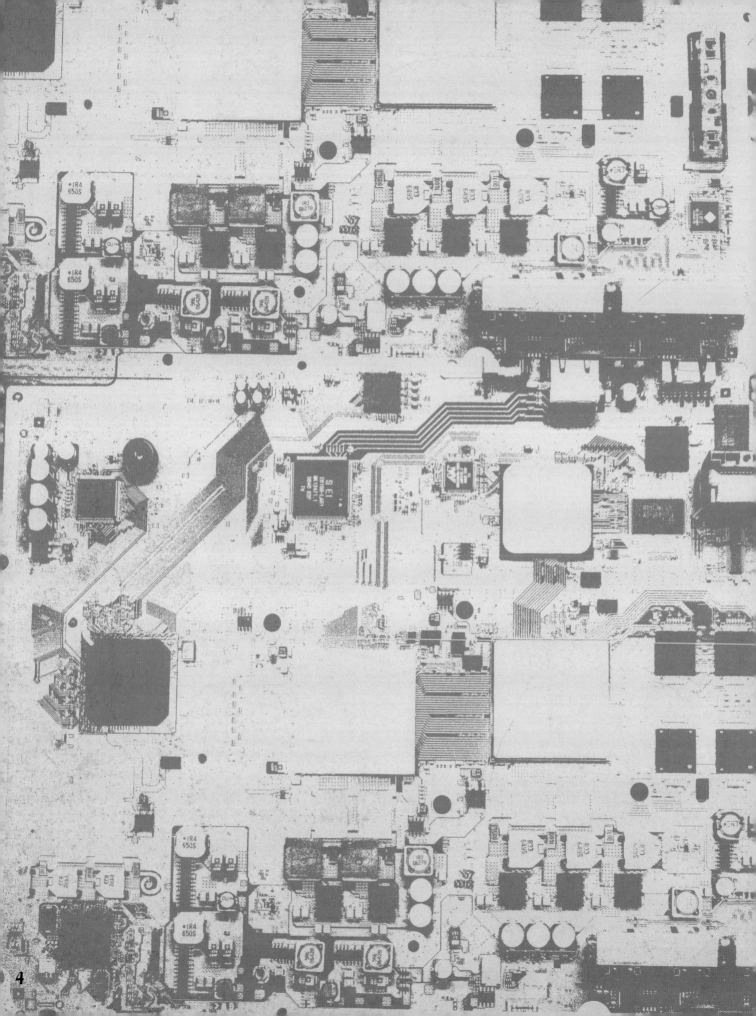

The two young space cadets, Eddie and Yelena, sat in the control room of the space ship. They were learning to be space rangers and were patrolling the universe, protecting Earth from attack. However, there was a problem. Eddie and Yelena were bored. "Nothing ever happens," said Yelena, yawning.

Suddenly the loud speakers interrupted.

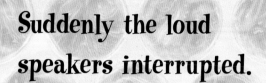

"Alert! Alert! Alien invasion!"

WARNING

Immediately the rangers sprang into action.

Eddie and Yelena followed
the rangers.

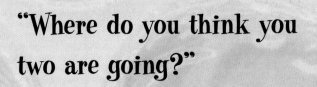

"Where do you think you
two are going?"

The Commander's voice stopped
the cadets in their tracks.

"To the ships," Eddie replied.

"To see off the aliens!"
Yelena added.

"Negative - this is no job for cadets. Stay here and guard the patrol ship."

"It's not fair," Yelena grumbled.

Eddie pointed to the panoramic viewing window.

"Anyway, it looks like the aliens are running away."

They watched the
alien spacecraft being
chased away by
the rangers.

KERCRUNCH!

The patrol ship shook, upending the cadets.

"What was that?"
asked Yelena.

"I don't know," said Eddie.

16

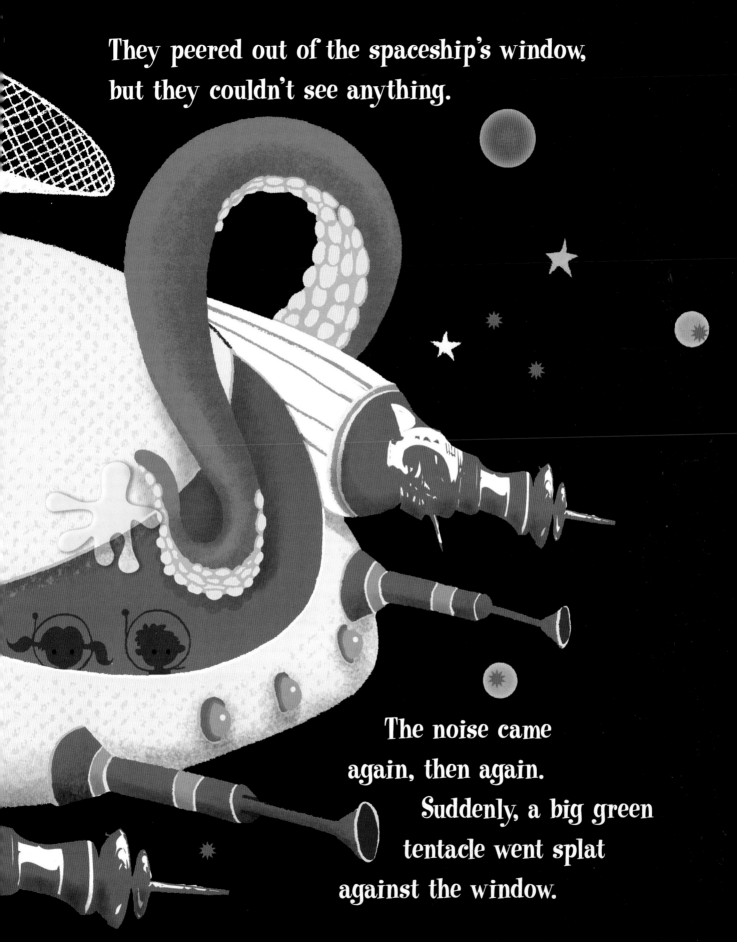

They peered out of the spaceship's window, but they couldn't see anything.

The noise came again, then again. Suddenly, a big green tentacle went splat against the window.

"Aliens!" cried Eddie.

"But how?" Yelena asked. "We saw them leave!"

"It must have been a trick!"
said Eddie.

"What do we do now?"
Yelena asked.

"Let's find out how many of
them there are," Eddie replied. "Scanners -
show the outside
of the ship."

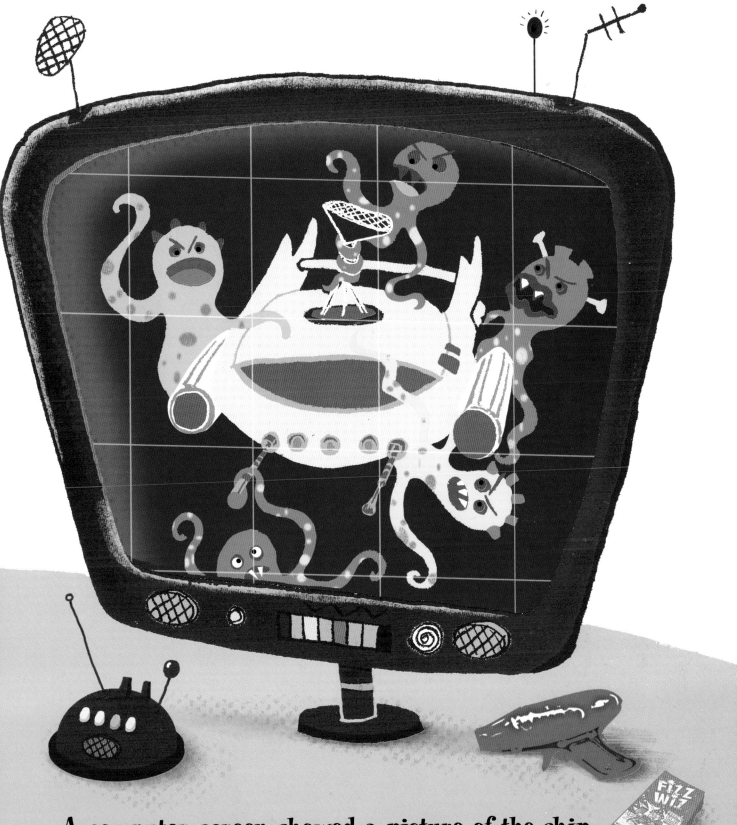

A computer screen showed a picture of the ship.
It was covered in monsters with tentacles.

"We're surrounded!" said Eddie.

"I've got a plan," said Yelena. "Eddie, get the escape pod ready - we're going to the Moon base."

"But what about the patrol ship?
If the aliens get it they could sneak
up on Earth and attack,"
Eddie said.

"Not if I press this."

Yelena pointed at a big red button.
The sign underneath said: "Danger! Self Destruct.
Do Not Press".

Eddie understood immediately. If Yelena pressed the button they would have twenty seconds to get away from the patrol ship before it blew up.

"OK," Eddie replied. "But we're going to get into big trouble for this."

"Not as big as letting the aliens get the patrol ship," Yelena replied.

MAJOR ALERT

"Good point," said Eddie. "I'll get the escape pod ready."

Yelena took a deep breath and pressed the button.

"Warning! Warning!

Self Destruct will begin in twenty seconds.
Nineteen. Eighteen..."

Yelena jumped into the
escape pod.

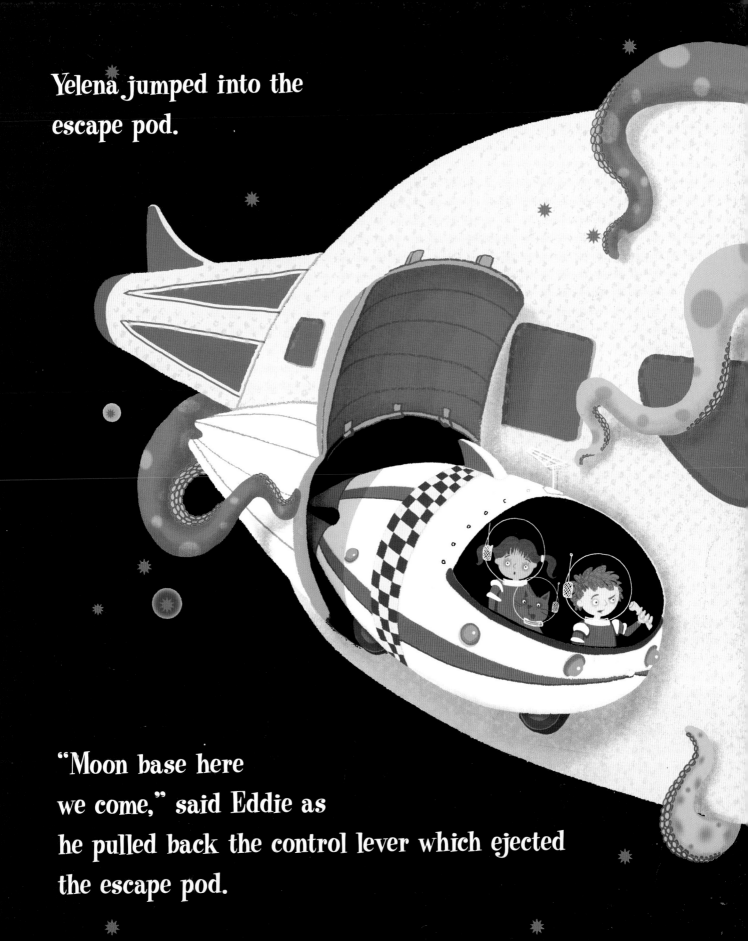

"Moon base here
we come," said Eddie as
he pulled back the control lever which ejected
the escape pod.

An enormous explosion disintegrated the patrol ship.

"I think we vaporized those aliens," said Yelena checking the computer monitor. "We saved the day!"

"Excellent job, Yelena," said Eddie. He brought their escape pod in to land. "But perhaps you can explain to the rangers why their patrol ship has disappeared!"

If you enjoyed this book, look out for another Take 2 title:

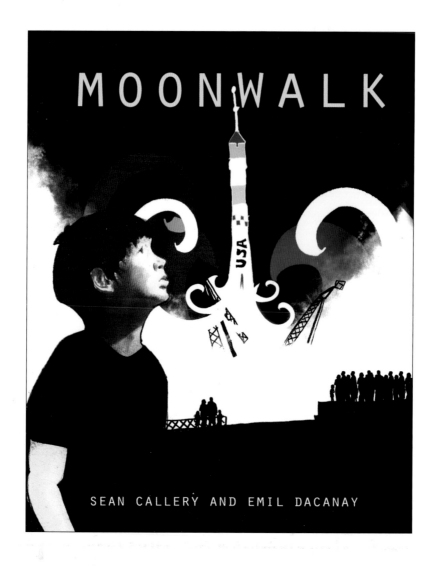

the dramatic story of the first moon landing told by Jay, whose dad works at the Space Center.